TULSA CITY-COUNTY LIBRARY

Dear Parents:

Congratulations! Your child is taking the first steps on an exciting journey. The destination? Independent reading!

STEP INTO READING® will help your child get there. The program offers five steps to reading success. Each step includes fun stories and colorful art or photographs. In addition to original fiction and books with favorite characters, there are Step into Reading Non-Fiction Readers, Phonics Readers and Boxed Sets, Sticker Readers, and Comic Readers—a complete literacy program with something to interest every child.

Learning to Read, Step by Step!

Ready to Read   Preschool–Kindergarten
• big type and easy words • rhyme and rhythm • picture clues
For children who know the alphabet and are eager to begin reading.

Reading with Help   Preschool–Grade 1
• basic vocabulary • short sentences • simple stories
For children who recognize familiar words and sound out new words with help.

Reading on Your Own   Grades 1–3
• engaging characters • easy-to-follow plots • popular topics
For children who are ready to read on their own.

Reading Paragraphs   Grades 2–3
• challenging vocabulary • short paragraphs • exciting stories
For newly independent readers who read simple sentences with confidence.

Ready for Chapters   Grades 2–4
• chapters • longer paragraphs • full-color art
For children who want to take the plunge into chapter books but still like colorful pictures.

STEP INTO READING® is designed to give every child a successful reading experience. The grade levels are only guides; children will progress through the steps at their own speed, developing confidence in their reading. The F&P Text Level on the back cover serves as another tool to help you choose the right book for your child.

Remember, a lifetime love of reading starts with a single step!

To Mom, baker of cakes.
And to Lance, eater of cakes.
—F.G.

Visit us on the Web!
StepIntoReading.com
rhcbooks.com

Educators and librarians, for a variety of teaching tools, visit us at RHTeachersLibrarians.com

Library of Congress Cataloging-in-Publication Data
Names: Gilbert, Frances, author. | Unten, Eren Blanquet, illustrator.
Title: I love cake! / by Frances Gilbert ; illustrated by Eren Unten.
Description: New York : Random House Children's Books, [2021] |
Series: Step into reading. Step 1 | Audience: Ages 4–6. | Audience: Grades K–1. |
Summary: "A little girl, with the help of her grandma, bakes her very first cake for her mom's birthday." —Provided by publisher.
Identifiers: LCCN 2020005819 (print) | LCCN 2020005820 (ebook) |
ISBN 978-0-593-30137-1 (trade paperback) | ISBN 978-0-593-30138-8 (library binding) |
ISBN 978-0-593-30139-5 (ebook)
Subjects: CYAC: Baking—Fiction. | Cake—Fiction. | Grandmothers—Fiction.
Classification: LCC PZ7.1.G547 Iac 2021 (print) | LCC PZ7.1.G547 (ebook) | DDC [E]—dc23

Printed in the United States of America

10 9 8 7 6 5 4 3 2 1

This book has been officially leveled by using the F&P Text Level Gradient™ Leveling System.

STEP INTO READING®

STEP 1

READY TO READ

I Love Cake!

by Frances Gilbert
illustrated by Eren Unten

Random House 🏠 New York

Today,
I am going to bake.
I am going to bake
a cake.

I like to crack
the eggs.
Crack, crack, crack!

I like to mix
the batter.
Mix, mix, mix!

I pour it
into the pans.

Grandma puts the
pans in the oven.
Now I have to wait!

I do not like to wait
for cake!
Bake, cake, bake!

Beep! Beep! Beep!

My cake is baked!

I want to

eat it now!

But first,
I need to frost
my cake.

I love pink frosting!

I also love
purple, blue, yellow,
and red frosting.

Perfect!

Now I need to
make my cake fancy.
It needs
strawberries.

It also needs
lollipops,

jelly beans,

and candy canes.

Perfect!

Now I need to
write words
on my cake.

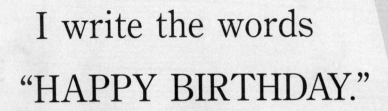

I write the words
"HAPPY BIRTHDAY."

Now I can eat
my cake!

Grandma puts my cake
on the table.

But my cake is
too big!

Oops!
My cake fell over!
But I still want
to eat it.

"Happy birthday, Mom!
I baked you a cake!"

I love my mom.
And I love cake!